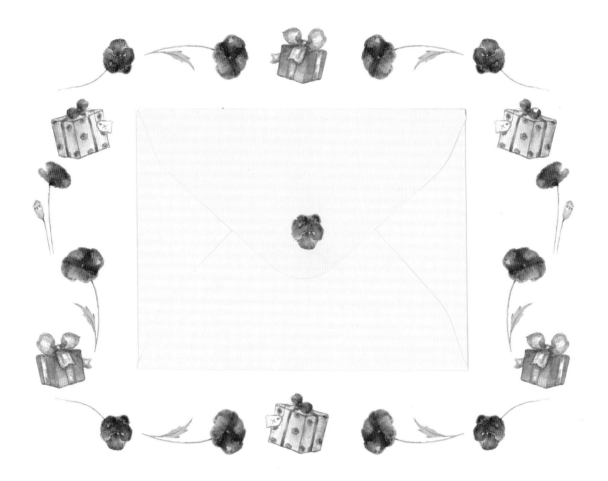

Honeypot Hill

← To the City

The Orchards

Saffron Thimble's Sewing Shop

Paddle Steamer Quay

Aunt Marigold's General Store

Lavender Valley Garden Centre

Healing House and Garden

The Worthingtons' House

Lavender Lake

Bumble Bee's Teashop

Lavender Lake School of Dance

Peppermint Pond

Hedgerows Hotel
Where Mimosa lives

SCHOOL

Rosehip School

Summer Meadow

Christmas Corner

Wildspice Woods

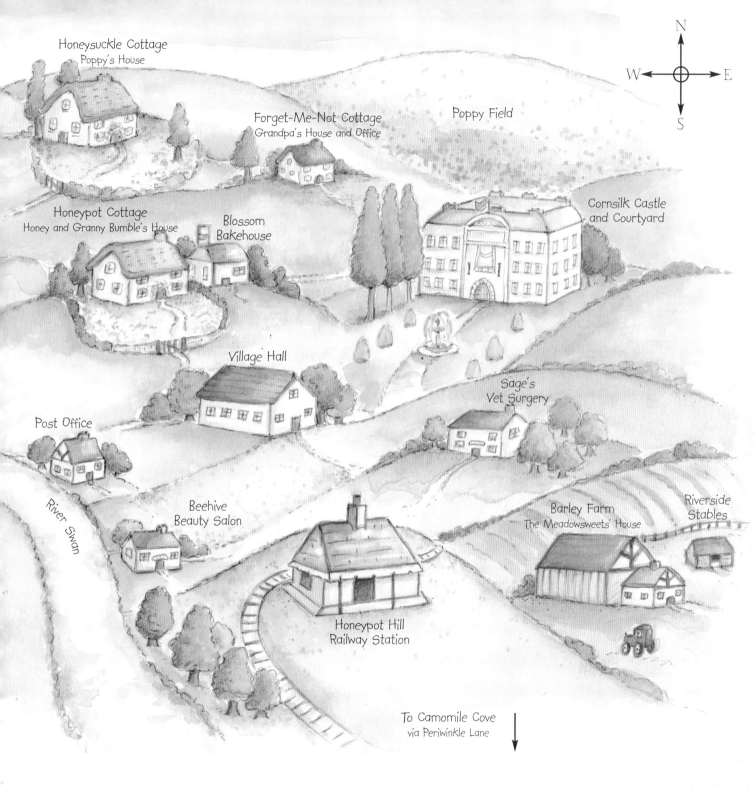

N
W   E
S

Honeysuckle Cottage
Poppy's House

Forget-Me-Not Cottage
Grandpa's House and Office

Poppy Field

Cornsilk Castle
and Courtyard

Honeypot Cottage
Honey and Granny Bumble's House

Blossom
Bakehouse

Village Hall

Sage's
Vet Surgery

Post Office

River Swan

Beehive
Beauty Salon

Barley Farm
The Meadowsweets' House

Riverside
Stables

Honeypot Hill
Railway Station

To Camomile Cove
via Periwinkle Lane

Join Princess Poppy on more adventures . . .

★ Ballet Shoes ★

★ Twinkletoes ★

★ The Fair Day Ball ★

THE BIRTHDAY
A PICTURE CORGI BOOK: 978 0 552 55800 6

First published in Great Britain by Picture Corgi,
an imprint of Random House Children's Books

This edition published 2006

7 9 10 8 6

Text copyright © Janey Louise Jones, 2006
Illustration copyright © Picture Corgi Books, 2006
Illustrations by Veronica Vasylenko
Design by Tracey Cunnell

Picture Corgi Books are published by Random House Children's Books,
61–63 Uxbridge Road, London W5 5SA,
a division of The Random House Group Ltd, in Australia by Random House Australia (Pty) Ltd,
20 Alfred Street, Milsons Point, Sydney, NSW 2061, Australia,
in New Zealand by Random House New Zealand Ltd,
18 Poland Road, Glenfield, Auckland 10, New Zealand,
and in South Africa by Random House (Pty) Ltd,
Isle of Houghton, Corner Boundary Road & Carse O'Gowrie, Houghton 2198, South Africa
THE RANDOM HOUSE GROUP Limited Reg. No. 954009
www.kidsatrandomhouse.co.uk
www.princesspoppy.com

A CIP catalogue record for this book is available from the British Library.

Printed in China

Princess Poppy

The Birthday

Written by Janey Louise Jones

PICTURE CORGI

For Emma Brown,
who was a true princess

The Birthday

featuring

Honey
★

Mum
★

Princess Poppy

Granny Bumble
★

Saffron Thimble
★

Grandpa
★

Dad
★

Poppy woke up early.

"YIPPEE! It's my birthday!" she shouted as she jumped out of bed.

"I love birthdays," said Poppy. "Today I can be a special princess all day long!"

Poppy looked around her room – toys, books and dressing-up clothes were scattered all over the place, but she couldn't see any sign of a present.

Hmmmm, nothing for a birthday princess in here.

"I do hope everyone has remembered my birthday," she sighed.

Poppy brushed her hair . . .

put on her favourite red dress . . .

and put her poppy hairclips on.

"I'm off to find my birthday things!" she announced,
and rushed off to her parents' room.

"Mum, Dad, I'm here," said Poppy.

"Oh, Poppy, I'm still sleepy," said a muffled voice from under the bedcovers.

"But it's my birth—" Poppy began.

"Go back to bed for half an hour," mumbled Mum.

"It *is* only seven o'clock in the morning, Poppy," groaned Dad.

"How could Mum and Dad sleep late on my special day?" wondered Poppy, crossly.

She went back to lie on her bed. "This is so boring," grumped the birthday girl.

So she decided to go next door and see Granny Bumble – she was always up early.

When Poppy arrived, there were lots of freshly chopped strawberries on the table and Granny Bumble was beating sugar and butter in a big bowl.

"Hello, Granny Bumble, it's my birth—"

"Poppy, can't you see I'm in the middle of something?

Run along now, I'll see you later," she smiled.

Even Granny Bumble doesn't care that it's my birthday.

"Right, that's it!" Poppy decided. "I'm going to see Grandpa. At least *he* would never forget my birthday."

Poppy walked through the big door into Grandpa's office
and found him hiding behind a huge newspaper.

"Can't talk, dear!" said Grandpa. "I'm stuck on my crossword!"

Poppy marched out and closed the door with a BANG!

Not Grandpa too.

"And his newspaper was upside down!" she said.

Next, Poppy peeped into the window of the sewing shop. Her cousin Saffron was busy stitching a beautiful red ball dress.

"Hi, Saffron, that looks gorgeous! Did you know it's—"

"Poppy, I'm sorry, but I've really got to get on with this job,"
said Saffron. "This is for a girl who can't wait for anything.
I don't have time to chat."

Even Saffron is too busy!

So Poppy went to the Lavender Garden to find her best friend Honey . . .

Honey was dressed up in her fairy outfit.

"Please tell me *you* have remembered my birthday," pleaded Poppy.

"Oh, Poppy, I haven't forgotten, but I haven't exactly remembered, if you see what I mean," said Honey, sounding a bit confused.

Poor Poppy felt so sad. It was as if no one cared enough about her to remember her special day.

"I just don't understand it," she said. "Mum *always* says I'm a special princess on my birthday."

Suddenly Honey jumped up. "Come with me, Poppy. Let's go and play in the courtyard."

As they got closer to the courtyard, they heard beautiful music playing.

Honey opened the gates . . .

"SURPRISE!"

Streamers, balloons and flower petals showered down on Poppy's head.

"Bang!" went the party poppers.

"Happy Birthday!" shouted Poppy's family and friends.

"WOW!" laughed Poppy.
"Thank you! You *have* remembered!"

"You've waited very patiently, darling," said Mum.

"Now you can open all your lovely presents!"

Mum gave Poppy a bright red velvet box.

Inside was a glittering necklace.

Poppy put it on.

"It's so sparkly! Thanks, Mum! Thanks, Dad!"

Granny Bumble stepped forward with a birthday sponge cake decorated with fresh strawberries and cream.

Poppy blew out the glowing candles, then she tasted a slice.

"Mmm, deeeelicious!"

Grandpa handed Poppy a gorgeous tiara with three poppies on it.
Poppy put it on.

"I love it! Thanks, Grandpa!"

Then Saffron gave Poppy a huge white box, covered in poppies, with a red bow on top.

Poppy opened the box, and pulled out a red princess ball dress and red velvet shoes.

"Oh, Saffron, it *was* for me! Thank you!" exclaimed Poppy.
"I thought you said it was for a girl who can't wait for anything!"

Everyone started to laugh.

"But Poppy," said Honey, "it's only just after breakfast time now and you *have* been finding it hard to wait for your presents, haven't you?"

"Maybe a little bit," giggled Poppy. "I should have known something lovely was going to happen."

Honey then handed her friend a small glass bottle with a red ribbon tied around it.

"It's petal perfume," Honey explained. "I made it myself."

"Oh, Honey, it smells lovely!" Poppy said as she dabbed the perfume behind her ears.

Then Poppy dashed off to try on her princess dress and red velvet shoes.

"Poppy, you are the most beautiful princess ever," said Grandpa as she showed off all her wonderful presents.

"Grandpa," Poppy asked, "is *every* little girl a princess?"

"Yes, Poppy, every girl is a princess, especially on her birthday!"

Poppy did a little twirl. "What a perfect Princess Poppy Party!"

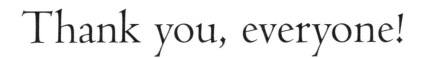

Thank you, everyone!